How Long Is Forever

How Long Is Forever

How Long Is Forever, Volume 1

Sakari Lacross

Published by Sakari Lacross, 2021.

Table of Contents

Chapter One 1

Chapter Two 5

Chapter Three 10

Chapter Four 16

Chapter Five 19

Chapter Six 24

Chapter Seven 30

Chapter Eight 36

Chapter Nine 42

Chapter Ten 48

Chapter Eleven 54

Chapter Twelve 59

Chapter Thirteen 67

Chapter Fourteen 73

Chapter Fifteen 77

Chapter Sixteen 82

Chapter Seventeen 88

Chapter Eighteen 93

Chapter Nineteen 102

Chapter Twenty 109

Chapter One

Movie night—the only time me and Mom had to spend together. It didn't bother me, though. Not like it used to. Being a single parent seemed quite difficult, leaving Mom with two jobs just to give us the average house we lived in. And no matter how many times I offered to help—meaning getting a job—she would tell me she'd rather I finish college.

So that was the deal: I go to college, and she works. Monday would be the first semester I attended. Mom wouldn't stop telling me how proud she was of me, even buying me my first car last week. It was used, something she bought from a friend who worked at a junkyard.

Tonight's movie was Stardust, a space movie about aliens attacking men on the moon—a movie she had been hyped about renting all week.

Sitting on the other end of the couch with my own blanket, I asked Mom the usual as the movie credits rolled.

"So, Mom, how was work today?"

Opening her bag of heated popcorn, she answered, "Not too bad. Dell didn't come in, so I earned a little extra for covering his shift. That's how I almost missed movie night with you."

"Oh," I replied, having nothing else to say as the movie started.

Movie night was my favorite night of the week. No matter how cheesy or lame the movie was, I could never tell Mom that—and believe me, this one was cheesy. But it wasn't about the movie. It was the only time she had for me.

On Saturdays, her first shift didn't start until the afternoon, so she could sleep in instead of leaving the house at six in the morning. I didn't wake up for school until seven, so I could never catch her to tell her to have a good day. So I started writing her notes, leaving them on the kitchen table the night before.

All we had... was each other.

Halfway through the movie, my mother drank two sodas. As usual, she paused the movie and called a five-minute intermission.

"Bathroom break," she announced, getting up from the sofa.

Heading down the hall, she went to the bathroom. Checking my cellphone, I saw it was now eleven at night. In another hour, my mom would be heading to bed. On weekdays, she would've been in bed an hour ago. The extra two hours mattered that much to us.

Breaking my train of thought, I heard glass shatter. Then—a chilling scream.

It was my mother's scream.

The sound came from the bathroom.

I jumped off the couch and sprinted down the hall. I grabbed the doorknob and wiggled it, but it wouldn't budge. The door was locked.

My forehead began to sweat as the screams continued, making my nerves worse as I slammed my shoulder against the door.

"I'm coming, Mom!!" I yelled as I kept hitting it.

Then I froze.

I heard a growl.

Not a dog's growl—but something monstrous. A sound I had never heard before. A growl that didn't belong to anything human.

My mind raced, trying to imagine what was on the other side of the door—when I suddenly realized... my mother was no longer screaming.

With one final, desperate hit, the door burst open.

The sight in front of me was horrific.

Glass from the bathroom window was shattered everywhere. Blood smeared across the floor and walls, leading to the open window.

But there was no sign of my mother.

She was gone.

One of her polka-dotted socks—and some kind of dagger—was left behind. The dagger was stained with blood.

It all happened so fast.

We... we were just watching a movie together.

The last movie night we would ever have.

Chapter Two

Three months had passed, and no one had any trace of where my mother was. No footprints... no hounds could pick up a trail... nothing. It didn't make any sense. How could someone carry another person away without leaving a trace in the snow? The police were as helpless as ever. What the hell was going on?

I wanted to be done with school. I wanted to be done with life—to end it with the knife I found in the bathroom.

The amount of pain I carried followed me everywhere I went. I had no safe place to escape it. Even on nights when I couldn't bring myself to sleep at home and stayed outside in the backyard shed, I couldn't numb the pain. Not even the harsh weather could do that for me.

It was spring now. The rain didn't fall often enough to wash the hurt off me—to wash away the visions of blood that filled my mind every time I closed my eyes. Some days, I didn't sleep at all, and the images of blood on my hands haunted me. Reality began to slip away.

The state paid for me to see a therapist. As expected, he was useless. I eventually stopped going. However, he did send me a letter in the mail, giving me an address to visit. In the letter, he claimed this place would be able to help me further. He even said they could assist me better than the police with my mother's disappearance.

Curiosity took hold of me, bringing me to the entrance of a school academy.

Standing at the locked gate, I waited for someone to let me in. After using the buzzer mounted on the wall, a man had told me someone would be coming shortly.

The scenery was unsettling. The school was cut off from society, hidden deep within the woods. The letter gave me specific directions to follow—otherwise, I would've been lost for who knows how long before ever finding this place.

Hearing a twig snap, I quickly turned around, prepared for anything that might've been sneaking up on me.

Gripping the dagger strapped to my side, I came face to face with a woman—a familiar face. If I wasn't mistaken, approaching me was—

"Dawn?" she spoke before I could.

Throwing her arms around me in a warm hug confirmed it. It was none other than my childhood friend, Luna—a girl who used to live next door when we were twelve, back when my parents were still together. She was my best friend.

She wasn't much taller than she had been back then, her long black hair still the same. I'd never forget the day I was forced to move away from her—the day my mother left my father for good.

Luna and I sat on her porch steps like we always did. But unlike her, I wasn't in a talkative mood. I couldn't hide my strange behavior for long before she finally asked,

"Is there something wrong?"

Using every ounce of strength in my small body, I held back the tears that threatened to fall. I paused, staring up at the midday sky—anything to avoid looking her in the eyes.

"We're leaving."

"What do you mean?"

"My mom... she's leaving my dad. I have to go with her."

"So... you're moving away?"

"Yeah. Today, actually. I guess this is the last time we'll get to hang out."

What had been a lonely hand resting between us was suddenly covered with warmth as Luna placed her hand over mine, drawing my attention back to her face. I could see she was holding back tears too.

"I thought I heard your parents arguing last night," she said, forcing a small smile.

"Sorry about that," I replied, attempting one of my own.

"Don't worry about it. At least you were still here. At least we could still hang out."

Her cheeks flushed slightly as her smile slowly faded.

Breaking the silence that followed, I heard my mom call my name. It was time to go.

"I have to leave now," I said.

Turning away, I slipped my hand from beneath hers—but before I could take another step, I felt warmth against my cheek.

It was her lips.

A goodbye kiss.

Then she ran back into the house.

That was seven years ago.

Looking at her now, as we pulled away from our hug, she hadn't changed much. Just like that day, I put on a front, avoiding telling her that my mother was missing—possibly dead by now.

"What are you doing here?" I asked.

"I go to school here," she said with a smile. "What are you doing here?"

"I was sent here by someone," I replied simply.

A guy around our age approached the gate—a young man with slicked-back hair and glasses. He pressed a button on his side, and the gate opened.

As Luna walked through, she glanced back at me.

"It was nice seeing you."

"Same here."

Chapter Three

Entering the gates, I followed the guy who led me to the principal's office. Sitting at his desk, he greeted me as I took a seat in the chair in front of him.

"Our expected guest, I presume?"

I nodded slightly. "Yes, I am. My therapist sent me."

Why the hell was I at a school? What did a school have to do with my mother's disappearance? Did the bastard who took her used to attend this place or something? None of this was adding up.

"If you were sent here, then it was for a reason you would have never guessed."

Opening his desk drawer, the principal pulled out a file of paperwork.

"What is your name?"

"Dawn," I said. "Dawn Baker."

He searched through the stack of papers before pulling out a packet and separating it from the rest.

"Here you are," he said, scanning the documents for a moment before continuing. "So, it seems your mother went missing three months ago. She was taken right out of your home?"

"Yes, sir." I kept my tone flat, hiding how sensitive the subject was.

The man paused, closing the file and resting his elbow on the desk, his hand lightly cupping his chin as he studied me.

"It's possible that what took your mother was none other than... a vampire."

A wave of confusion washed over me, quickly turning into disbelief—and irritation.

"Is this some kind of joke?" I snapped. "A prank or something? What kind of therapist do I have?"

The principal's expression didn't change. He remained serious—almost too serious, like a machine.

Now uneasy, I stood from my chair and moved toward the door.

"That dagger on your hip," the man said, stopping me in my tracks, "is called a hunter's weapon. It is designed to kill vampires—crafted by hunters and blessed by witches."

I turned back around and approached his desk again, this time remaining on my feet.

"First you tell me vampires kidnapped my mother, now you're telling me witches exist? What's wrong with you?" I confronted him.

Looking up at me, his hands now folded on the desk, he replied calmly,

"People often fear the truth. Just because something is unknown to you does not mean it doesn't exist."

"Then show me a vampire," I challenged, calling his bluff.

He said nothing.

After a few seconds, I turned back toward the door—only to realize the student who had opened the gate was now standing directly behind me.

Confused, I frowned. I could've sworn he had been standing by the door. I hadn't heard him move at all. Maybe he was just light on his feet... or maybe I needed to ease up on the medication the clinic had given me.

"Excuse me," I said, trying to step around him.

He grabbed my arm.

I froze, shooting him a look that clearly told him to let go. He didn't. Instead, he smiled.

A smile that sent chills down my spine—familiar chills. The same ones I felt the night my mother was taken.

Then he showed me his teeth.

They were perfect... except for two on the top row.

They were longer. Sharper.

Fangs.

My eyes widened, frozen like a deer in headlights.

"Do you believe me now?" the principal's voice echoed behind me.

The vampire released my arm, but I couldn't look away. Slowly, my body turned back toward the desk.

"Th-those are real?" I stammered. "That's... a real vampire?"

"Yes," the principal replied. "As I said before, vampires exist."

"Are you a vampire too?"

"No. Like you, I am human. This academy was built to bring humans and vampires together."

My lips parted, but no words came out. The cold grip of fear held my body in place as I slowly sank back into the chair.

The principal stood, pacing slowly as he continued.

"Vampires have always lived among us. They've been involved in countless mysterious and unsolved cases. However, hunters have also existed—humans who eliminate the supernatural. Vampires, rogue witches... even werewolves, back when they still roamed."

"Serves those mutts right," the student behind me muttered.

"The hunters eventually realized too much blood was being shed. Most vampires only want to survive—to feed, just as humans must eat to live. So, a group of hunters created this school. Protected by witch magic, only invited humans and supernatural beings can find this place. Anyone else who enters these woods would wander endlessly, never discovering it."

"So why invite humans to live on a campus with—"

I glanced back at the vampire behind me for a split second before finishing,

"—killers?"

"Because these vampires and humans represent the future of our society. Proof that vampires are not our enemies, but evolved beings who simply want to live. They are not killers—only survivors. Like the Lycans, they do not wish to face extinction."

"Then why am I here?" I pressed. "How is this place supposed to help me find the vampire who took my mother?"

"We brought you here for our own reasons. Most vampires who attack humans do not leave survivors. They prefer to remain hidden. The fact that you're alive is... unusual. There must be a reason you were spared. That vampire could have killed both of you in less than a minute."

"So what's your reason? None of this makes sense. You're saying vampires don't leave survivors, but here I am—alive. Meanwhile, my mother is out there being some bloodsucker's meal!"

"Offensive much?" the vampire behind me muttered.

Ignoring him, the principal continued,

"We can try to help you find your mother. But it's important that every survivor of a vampire encounter remains at this school—for their own safety."

"And how long am I supposed to stay here?"

"This will be your permanent home."

I shook my head. "No thanks."

Standing again, I walked toward the door.

"We have your records," the principal said calmly. "We can find you again. If you leave, we will terminate you to protect the secrecy of the supernatural world. Hunter protocol."

I stopped.

"You will be killed within twenty-four hours of leaving the school grounds."

Chapter Four

Three months had passed, and by force, I remained at the academy. I lived in the human dorm, which was on the opposite side of campus. Hunters and huntresses in training were assigned to both dorms, ensuring balance between vampires and humans without death or violence.

There were three rules to attending the school. First, humans were not allowed to interact with vampires without hunter supervision. Second, vampires were not allowed to feed on humans. Third, vampires were never allowed in the human dorm—ever.

Walking down the hallway toward my dorm room, my roommate, Hendrix, opened the door. To be honest, he was a bit of a dork—glasses, shirt neatly tucked into his pants, always studying or watching anime—the whole package. But he was a good guy.

"Dawn, did you hear about the party Al is throwing?" he asked as I stepped inside.

"No, I didn't," I replied.

"We should go," he suggested. "Lisa's going to be there."

"Really?" I smirked, glancing back at him as I set my backpack down in my room. "You should go without me. I've got a lot of extra credit work to catch up on."

The dorm rooms were set up like small two-bedroom apartments, with a shared kitchen and bathroom.

Hendrix stood at the end of the hallway that led into the living room.

"I'll do your work for you, buddy," he offered.

The desperation in his face matched the tone in his voice. Moments like this made it hard to tell him no.

I sighed. "Hendrix, we agreed you wouldn't do my work anymore. You don't have to cheat for me just so we can hang out or be friends."

Hendrix wasn't used to having friends. Truthfully, I was his first roommate who didn't bully him or treat him like trash. He had never even been kissed by a girl before—aside from his mother.

Like me, he had lost his mother to a vampire. The only difference was that he witnessed it—the vampire draining her.

What the vampire didn't know was that Hendrix's parents were hunters. His father killed it and sent Hendrix here to keep him safe from others.

"Tell you what," I said, "if you let me dress you, I'll go to the party with you tonight."

The smile on his face was impossible to describe. It was like watching a kid on his way to an amusement park.

"You've got it, buddy," Hendrix replied, practically sprinting into his room.

Closing my door, I got to studying. I was behind in math—the worst subject of all. I only had three days to finish all the extra credit work assigned to me.

Eighteen pages of homework stood between me and a passing grade.

But I brought this on myself.

Chapter Five

Nightfall arrived. Accompanying Hendrix, we walked across the campus grounds toward Al's dorm.

"Tonight is the night, Dawn. Tonight is the night I get a kiss from Lisa," Hendrix said, full of energy.

"I believe you, pal," I encouraged. "I know you can do it. You're finally going to make your move and win her over. Show her you deserve her just as much as anyone else. Remember—confidence and perseverance win girls over."

Nodding rapidly, Hendrix replied, "Got it."

Something in the distance caught my eye—two figures walking. Vampires. They were on their side of campus.

I stopped.

Hendrix stopped with me. My eyes stayed locked on them as they walked without a care in the world.

"Go to the party, Hendrix. I'll catch up with you."

"What?"

"I said I'll catch up. I've got something to do."

Hendrix stepped in front of me, placing both hands on my shoulders, blocking my view.

"Are you serious? Are you really about to do what I think you are?"

"I have to, Hendrix. The academy hasn't found anything about my mother. Maybe those bloodsuckers know something."

"Dawn, do you really want to—"

"I'll be fine," I cut him off. "Trust me. It won't take long. I'll meet you there."

He hesitated, studying my face. Then he nodded and walked away. He looked back twice... then not again.

As always, my dagger was strapped to my hip, tucked beneath my belt.

I approached the vampires quickly, glancing around to make sure no hunters were nearby. Crossing the boundary, I stepped out of the human domain and into vampire territory.

They noticed immediately.

The moment I crossed over, they turned toward me, picking up my scent.

In a blur, they rushed me—closing the distance instantly.

"What is a human doing over here?" one of them demanded. "Were you not taught the school's rules?"

They kept a short distance between us—close enough to threaten, far enough for me to react if needed.

This was my first real confrontation with vampires outside of the one in the office. Like all of them, they looked human. Young. Perfect skin.

"I've been here for about three months," I said, keeping my voice steady. My heart pounded as adrenaline surged through me. "I have questions about my mother—and you're going to give me answers. She was taken by your kind."

The long-haired vampire stepped back as the short-haired one moved forward.

That was my cue. My hand drifted toward my dagger.

"Are you trying to start trouble, human?" he asked.

"Quinton, don't," the long-haired one warned.

Quinton's pupils flashed red for a split second, attempting to intimidate me.

"Am I scaring you?" I taunted. "Does a pathetic human's presence threaten your non-beating heart?"

Quinton smirked, letting out a short chuckle.

Then—he vanished.

Before I could react, his hand was around my throat.

With barely any effort, he launched me through the air like I weighed nothing. I hit the ground hard, sliding several feet across the dirt—still within vampire territory.

I reached for my dagger—but he was already on me again.

He grabbed me and threw me even farther, my body rolling across the ground after impact.

Trying to anticipate his speed, I jumped up and threw a punch into the air, expecting him to appear in front of me.

He didn't.

Instead, I felt a finger tap my shoulder from behind.

I spun around, throwing another punch—but he dodged effortlessly, leaning back just enough for my fist to miss.

Then he countered.

His punch landed hard against my face, snapping my head to the side. Before I could recover, two more hits followed—fast, brutal. A fourth punch dropped me to the ground.

I lay on my side, dazed.

Quinton knelt beside me as I spat blood onto the dirt. He looked down at me like I was nothing.

"What a shame," he said calmly.

"Quinton, that's enough! You don't need another write-up!" the long-haired vampire shouted from a distance.

Quinton glanced back. "One more won't hurt! I know I always say that, but this time I mean it!"

I managed to grab my dagger.

As he turned back toward me, I swung—

And connected.

Quinton let out a sharp shout, stumbling back.

He retaliated instantly—driving a kick into my ribs that sent me crashing into a tree. I hit the ground moments later, pain exploding through my body.

He stepped back again, putting distance between us.

From where I lay, I could see him clutching his face.

"Damn it," he growled. "That's a hunter's dagger. The wound won't heal quickly... it's burning."

"Imagine if that hit your head," the long-haired vampire replied.

"He got lucky," Quinton snapped. "Faster than a normal human. Beginner's luck. That blade should've never touched me."

My vision blurred.

Pain consumed my body as I struggled to stay conscious.

But I couldn't hold on.

Everything faded.

And then—darkness.

Chapter Six

The warmth of a gentle touch against my face pulled me awake. My vision cleared to reveal Luna sitting in front of me. We were both on the floor of her living room, my body just recovering from unconsciousness.

"Luna," I called out as my vision spun briefly around the room, confirming I was in her dorm. "How did I end up here?"

Worry filled her expression as she answered immediately. "You were right outside my door—unconscious. Someone knocked, and when I opened it... it was just you."

The realization hit me instantly. The vampires had brought me here.

The thought of being carried by one of them made my blood boil, even if I didn't show it.

"Are you okay?" Luna asked, her concern deepening. "Who did this to you?"

"I'm fine," I said, pushing myself up slowly—only to feel a sharp pain in my ribs.

It was enough to make me grab my side instinctively.

"Don't sit up so fast," she warned. "Your ribs might be fractured."

Pain spread through my battered body, causing sweat to form on my skin despite the cool air from the A/C.

That's when I noticed—my shirt was off, replaced with bandages wrapped around my chest and stomach.

"Thanks for taking care of me," I said, already knowing the answer. I refused to give the vampires credit.

"Anytime," Luna replied softly. "Let's just hope this doesn't become a habit."

But the worry in her eyes didn't fade.

"Dawn... who did this to you?"

I knew she wouldn't let it go. Letting out a breath, I gave in.

"It was a vampire."

"A vampire? What were they doing on this side of campus?"

My silence answered for me.

Her expression shifted—from worry to disappointment.

I felt like a kid again.

"Now, Luna, let me explain—" I started.

"You let the school handle your mother's case, Dawn!" she snapped. "Don't go playing detective like that—they could've killed you!"

Her outburst startled me, sending another wave of pain through my body as I flinched.

Almost instantly, her tone softened. Her hands hovered near my chest, hesitant.

"I'm sorry," she said quietly. "I just... want you to be careful. The rules exist for a reason. The school will handle your mother's case."

"When?" I muttered through clenched teeth. "It's been three months, and I haven't gotten a single lead. Not one update."

"Things take time," Luna said gently. "There are a lot of people here dealing with situations like yours."

Her voice dropped near the end.

I caught it immediately.

"Luna... what happened to you? Why are you here?"

She didn't answer right away. She sat still, as if debating whether to speak.

"Maybe another time," I added, respecting her silence.

"No," she said quickly, raising her hand. "I'll tell you. Better now than never."

She took a breath.

"Before I came here, I had a little brother. His name was Marty. I was supposed to be watching him one night while my mom cooked. She realized she was missing an ingredient—some kind of seasoning—and went to the store. She told me to watch him... and the food."

Luna paused, her voice tightening.

"I was studying and cooking at the same time… so I didn't notice… I didn't notice he went outside."

Her voice began to crack.

"I still don't know why he did. But then… I heard him scream."

She swallowed hard.

"It was a scream that stuck with me… like he was dying."

Tears streamed down her face now.

"And he was. By the time I got there, it was too late. The front door was open… and he was lying on the doorstep. Cold."

Her voice dropped to barely a whisper.

"The bloodsucker didn't even let him turn… His neck was broken."

She broke down.

Without thinking, I pulled her into my arms. Her head pressed against my chest as her tears soaked into my bandages.

I said nothing at first—just held her, rubbing her back slowly.

"It wasn't your fault," I said quietly.

"Tell that to my mom," she cried. "She was destroyed after that. She couldn't take care of herself… let alone me. She gave me up for adoption four months later."

Her voice steadied slightly as she pulled back, wiping her tears. I helped her brush away what remained.

"If it wasn't for this academy... I don't know where I'd be. I turned eighteen the same month they found me. And... that was it."

Silence filled the room.

What was I supposed to say? There was no fix for this. No solution for people like us.

Everyone here had been broken by the same kind of nightmare—just to be forced to live alongside it.

What a joke.

Still, I spoke honestly.

"This sucks," I said. "We're stuck on a campus with the things that destroyed our lives. I wish I could change that. I wish I could save people. I wish I could've been there—for you... for my mom... for your brother."

I looked at her.

"You didn't deserve that. None of you did. And if no one's told you before... I'm sorry. And what happened to your brother... it's not going to happen to you."

"How do you know?" Luna asked quietly. "What makes you so sure? What makes you think these vampires won't lose control and come after us? We're basically trapped in a slaughterhouse."

I gently lifted her chin, making sure she looked directly at me.

I needed her to see I meant it.

"That's because I'm not just going to sit back," I said. "If this is a slaughterhouse... then I'll be the wolf that fights back. I'll take them down before they can hurt me—or anyone I care about."

My hand remained against her face.

She didn't pull away.

Silence settled between us again—but this time, it felt different.

Heavier.

Closer.

Our eyes stayed locked, and something shifted between us. I couldn't explain it—but I felt it. And somehow, I knew she did too.

She believed me.

Slowly, she leaned closer.

And without thinking...

I leaned in too.

Chapter Seven

Luna was all I had left. The kiss she gave me when we were kids—I never got the chance to return it.

Not until tonight.

Her lips were just as warm as they had been seven years ago. Only now, she wore lip gloss. A faint cherry scent filled my senses as passion drew my lips to hers.

My eyes closed as I silently wished under the moonlight that time would freeze—that we would remain like this forever, like a statue locked in a single moment.

But it didn't happen that way.

As much as I didn't want it to end, I pulled away the moment I felt my phone vibrating in my pocket.

I slowly leaned back, my eyes opening before hers. She looked down toward the floor, facing away from me—toward her bed.

I checked my phone.

A message from Hendrix.

Where are you, bro? Please don't tell me the vamps turned you into a snack.

At the end, he added a frowning face.

That was my cue.

I leaned forward, trying to slide off Luna's bed—but a sharp pain shot through my ribs, forcing a grunt from my throat.

Luna immediately leaned toward me, her hands hovering, ready to help.

"Dawn, you shouldn't move yet," she said.

I looked up at her, noticing her gaze fixed on the bandages wrapped around my torso.

"I know," I admitted. "But it's getting late. I should head back."

Suddenly, a wave of hunger hit me.

Sharp. Sudden.

It felt like I hadn't eaten in days—which made no sense. I had eaten just a few hours ago.

Luna suddenly looked up at me—and screamed.

She fell off the bed, scrambling backward across the floor, putting distance between us. Her eyes were locked onto mine, filled with pure fear. A look I had never seen from her before.

"What? What's wrong?" I asked, panic rising in my voice.

"Y-your eyes..." she stammered. "Th-they're... red. Like a vampire's."

She backed herself against the wall, her body trembling.

My own hands began to shake as her words sank in.

My eyes... were red?

Like a vampire's?

Why would she say that? Why would she be this afraid—unless she was telling the truth?

Before I could process it further, Luna reached the bedroom door.

"You... you can stay in here tonight," she said softly, before quickly stepping out and closing the door behind her.

Her expression lingered in my mind.

That fear... it felt real. Too real.

What was happening to me?

I didn't sleep that night.

I watched the sunrise from her room, my thoughts racing. From the sounds in the kitchen, Luna hadn't slept either.

A knock came at the door.

Soft. Careful.

It had to be her.

I hesitated. I didn't know what seeing my eyes like that had done to her. Did she see me as a monster now? Did she fear me the same way everyone feared the creatures at this school?

I didn't feel like a monster. I still felt human. I didn't drink blood. I had never even been bitten. So why were my eyes changing?

After a moment, I opened the door.

No one was there.

But across the living room, I could see light coming from the other bedroom.

She must've knocked... then gone back before I answered.

I must've scared her more than I thought.

Still... I needed her to know I was still me. Still human.

Maybe she had just imagined it. There was no way I could be anything else.

I left quietly, closing her apartment door behind me. No one saw me leave.

I moved quickly down the long, empty hallway before anyone could step out and spot me.

Once outside, the sunlight hit me hard.

It felt stronger than usual—almost unbearable, like the peak of summer heat. But it was only September.

What the hell was going on?

My skin tingled slightly, irritated, but not enough to stop me. Nothing a little sunscreen couldn't fix.

I made my way back toward the boys' dorm—the human dorm.

Halfway there, I instinctively reached for my hip.

My stomach dropped.

The dagger was gone.

Only the empty sheath remained.

The last thing my mother left behind.

I couldn't leave it.

But I couldn't go to the principal... or security. That would mean exposing what I did.

Which left me with only one option.

Go back.

Back into vampire territory.

And get it myself.

A suicide mission, considering how badly I got beaten last night—with the dagger. Now I had nothing.

What could I possibly do?

My phone vibrated again.

Hoping it was Luna, I pulled it out.

Hendrix. Calling.

"Sorry, man," I muttered. I didn't have time. Not right now.

I declined the call and powered my phone off completely.

It was daytime.

Which meant I had an advantage.

The vampires were probably asleep.

If I was going to get my dagger back…

Now was the only chance I had.

Chapter Eight

With fear lingering in my steps, I did my best not to show it as I approached the vampire dorm. Unlike the human side, there were very few people around. The few that were visible were clearly campus security—hunters patrolling the area while the vampires rested.

I managed to stay undetected, reaching the front entrance of the dorm near where I had fought the night before. My dagger had to be inside. It was no longer on the ground.

I knocked carefully—loud enough to be heard, but not enough to echo outside.

No answer.

I waited as long as I could, hoping campus security wouldn't circle back anytime soon. My heart pounded—not at the thought of a vampire opening the door, but at the thought of getting caught.

Then the door opened.

But it wasn't a vampire.

It was campus security.

I was screwed.

My eyes widened at the uniform she wore, instantly recognizing her authority. Short blue jean shorts, a white

T-shirt, and a cropped denim jacket—that was the standard for female campus security.

She looked around my age—maybe nineteen—but the expression on her face said everything.

She meant business.

"You're not a vampire," she said flatly. "The sun would've taken care of that by now. So give me one good reason why I shouldn't drag you to the discipline office."

My nerves spiked, but I forced myself to stay composed. Without thinking, I blurted out the first thing that came to mind.

"One of the bloodsuckers here has my dagger. I want it back."

I tried to sound confident—like I wasn't already in trouble.

She didn't budge.

"That's impossible," she replied. "The only way someone in this dorm would have your property is if you entered their dorm—or they entered yours. Both are violations of school policy."

She narrowed her eyes.

"Is there something you want to tell me?"

I froze.

Not a word came out.

There was no way I was admitting what I did. No way I was confessing to breaking one of the most important rules—especially after getting my ass handed to me because of it.

"I didn't think so," she said. "Now leave. And for the record, I'll be notifying security to make sure you don't come back here. This is your only warning."

She started to close the door.

I reacted without thinking—jamming my foot into the doorway to stop it.

Her eyes dropped to my foot.

Her expression didn't change.

Then—

The door flew open.

Her fist followed.

It slammed into my nose before I could react. The hit sent me straight to the ground, landing hard on my back.

Pain exploded through my face as I clutched my nose.

She stepped outside, closing the distance between us.

"I love it when students get out of line," she said, cracking her knuckles inside her blue fingerless gloves. "In my reports, I call it resisting instructions. That gives me the right to use force."

She smirked slightly.

"Right now, you're in danger—being on the vampire side of campus. So allow me to beat you back to safety."

She stood over me, almost enjoying this.

I was still sore from last night. In no condition to fight.

But I wasn't about to just lay there and get beaten down.

I pushed myself up, standing face to face with her again, wiping the blood from my nose.

I braced myself.

This time, I was ready—

Nope.

Another punch slammed into my nose.

Blood sprayed as I staggered backward, nearly collapsing again—but she grabbed my shirt, holding me upright.

A rapid punch to my stomach followed.

Then an uppercut to my forehead.

The world spun.

I hit the ground again.

Her hits were too fast. Too strong.

There was nothing normal about her.

What were they doing to these hunters?

I lay there for a moment, staring up at the sun, my thoughts spiraling.

What am I doing?

I'm really getting beaten up like this?

Girl… guy… whatever—this was ridiculous.

Sure, I was already weakened from last night—but I shouldn't have been this outmatched.

Something wasn't right.

"Had enough yet?" she asked, standing over me again.

I forced myself up, pain radiating through my entire body.

Still, I smirked.

"I… want my mother's dagger," I said through strained breath. "It's all I have left of her."

"Give it up, kid," she replied. "You're not going to guilt me. I'm less human than you think."

I steadied myself again.

Waiting.

She didn't keep me waiting long.

She swung—fast.

But this time...

I saw it.

The punch slowed.

Not actually—but it felt slower.

Like time itself was stretching.

I even had a moment to glance past her—to the second-floor window of the dorm.

A student stood there.

Watching.

Expressionless.

Then my focus snapped back.

I grabbed her wrist mid-swing—stopping her punch completely.

The force behind it was still there. I could feel it. But it never reached me.

Her eyes widened slightly.

For the first time... she looked surprised.

"It seems," she said slowly, "you're less human than I thought."

Chapter Nine

"There is no untrained human who has ever been able to stop the velocity of my blows. Half the vampires here can't even defend themselves against my speed without fleeing. So tell me... do you also drink vampire blood?"

Her question made my stomach turn. Nausea rose instantly, threatening to make me vomit. For a moment, it even distracted me from the pain pulsing through my body.

"Also?" I repeated, letting go of her wrist.

"Yes," she answered. "I drink vampire blood."

The nausea worsened. I wasn't prepared for what she was telling me.

"I was born with a rare blood type that makes me immune to the poison in a vampire's fangs—the same poison that allows them to turn their victims. Because of that, I chose to become the ultimate hunter... to protect those less fortunate than me."

She continued, calm and matter-of-fact.

"So I used my gift to consume their strength. Fortunately for me, their blood adapted well to my body. It gave me their speed... their power... without their weaknesses."

I stood frozen, staring at her.

"I used that power to survive," she went on, "until I enrolled at this academy. That's when I realized strength alone wasn't enough. Now I serve as campus security—just like any other hunter here."

She paused briefly.

"I was assigned to the vampire division."

I didn't move.

Didn't speak.

I just stood there, trying to process everything she had said.

The woman turned her back to me and began walking away.

"I'll let you off this time," she said over her shoulder. "But don't come back. Next time... it won't end the same."

She cracked her knuckles again.

"Name's Karma. And trust me—you don't want that name following you around this campus."

Karma.

Yeah... I wasn't going to forget that.

On my way back, her words stayed with me.

I was starting to understand just how far humans were willing to go to survive in a world like this. I couldn't decide if Karma was one of the lucky ones... or completely insane. She carried the strengths of vampires, the will of a human—and the mindset of something in between.

Something adaptive.

Something dangerous.

The lines were blurring.

The difference between human and vampire didn't feel so clear anymore.

Maybe Karma was the answer to what was happening to me.

Maybe... somehow... I had vampire blood in me too.

Just... not in the same way.

What if I didn't drink it?

What if I was born with it already in my system? Enough to give me their abilities—but not turn me into one of them.

That didn't sound so bad.

Right?

Would that be enough for Luna to understand? To see that I wasn't a monster?

...Who was I kidding?

She'd still see me as one.

Maybe it was better to keep that to myself.

The bell rang, signaling the end of daytime classes. Evening had arrived.

The sun hung low in the sky as the campus shifted.

Day students began heading back to their dorms, while night classes started to open.

Humans and vampires moved along their respective sides of campus, with only hunters crossing between both. I walked with the crowd of humans, watching as they stared at the vampires.

Some looked afraid.

Others... fascinated.

This was one of the only times during the day when both sides saw each other. The other being just before sunrise—when vampires returned to their dorms and humans prepared for morning classes.

I glanced toward the night students.

The vampires.

For a moment, I wondered...

Should I be over there?

Or here?

What was I?

I can answer that.

The voice cut through everything.

I stopped walking, looking around—but no one else reacted. No one else heard it.

Nobody can hear me except you, the voice continued. I'm speaking directly into your mind.

"What do you want?" I whispered. "Why are you in my head? Where are you?"

Meet me in Building J.

The voice was calm. Controlled.

I'm heading there now. I'll make sure it's clear for you.

A pause.

And I'll make sure your weapon is returned to you.

I hesitated.

Trusting a voice without a face?

That sounded like a terrible idea.

I scanned the crowd, searching for anything unusual—but everyone moved normally. No one stood out.

Still...

I needed my mother's dagger back.

And so far...

I'd managed to survive worse.

...Kind of.

This wouldn't be any different.

Right?

Chapter Ten

I snuck along the outskirts of the campus as it began to clear out, avoiding open areas where I could easily be spotted. It didn't take long to reach Building J, located on the western edge of the school, near the back.

This was still vampire territory—but as promised, there were no hunters or vampires in sight.

The only problem?

The vampire who had been speaking to me wasn't in sight either.

I stood beside the building, keeping myself out of the open as much as possible. My eyes scanned the area, searching for whoever had called me here.

"Damn it," I muttered, growing more anxious by the second.

Just being here made me uneasy. If a hunter caught me, I'd definitely be punished. Karma had let me off easy—but there was no guarantee anyone else would.

"Sorry for the wait."

A calm, emotionless voice spoke from behind me.

I turned instantly.

Standing in front of me was a pale man—around my age, with flawless skin. His light pink hair brushed his shoulders, and his lavender eyes were unlike anything I had ever seen on a vampire before.

His expression was almost nonexistent.

Cold.

Perfect.

Too perfect to be human.

In his right hand, he held something wrapped in cloth. He extended it toward me.

I hesitated.

"Go ahead," he said softly, his voice sending a chill through me. "I won't harm you."

I didn't trust him. Not for a second.

He was a vampire—and they brought nothing but harm.

But he had my dagger.

So I took the risk.

Approaching cautiously, I closed the distance and quickly snatched the object from his hand. Pulling away immediately, I unwrapped it—

My dagger.

I stepped back, putting space between us again, watching him closely. He simply stared at me with that same eerie, emotionless look.

I broke the silence.

"What—are you expecting a thank you?"

He didn't answer right away. He just kept staring.

It made my skin crawl.

"That would be nice," he finally said, raising his hands slightly. "Considering I burned both of them retrieving your weapon."

He wasn't lying.

His palms were badly burned—most of the skin damaged.

"They were worse before," he added. "The healing has already begun."

For a moment, I felt something unfamiliar.

Sympathy.

Like seeing someone broken... struggling... even if they didn't deserve it.

I pushed the feeling away.

"Why haven't they healed yet?" I asked.

He lowered his hands.

"That blade is a hunter's weapon," he explained. "The only type capable of killing vampires with ease. Because it's blessed by witches, it carries an aura that suppresses our natural abilities—including our healing."

He paused.

"In simple terms... it affects us the way normal weapons affect humans."

"You don't say," I replied.

"I was told that weapon belonged to your mother," he continued. "Was she a hunter?"

"What's it to you?"

"Just curiosity. Hunter weapons are not easy to obtain. They are not sold. A human must pass a hunter trial to earn one—and even then, it must be granted by a witch, with approval from a grandmaster hunter."

I had been ready to leave.

But now...

I stayed.

Because for the first time, I realized something.

I didn't know much about my mother at all.

Maybe she had been hiding more than I thought.

Maybe... she was a hunter.

I decided to take advantage of this.

"So if what you're saying is true," I said, "my mother could only have gotten this weapon by becoming a hunter? There's no way someone just gave it to her?"

"No," he replied. "It is forbidden for a hunter to give their weapon to a non-hunter. It is also forbidden for another hunter to wield a weapon that isn't theirs."

He studied me.

"But since you are not a hunter, I understand why the principal allowed you to keep it."

A pause.

"You are barely even human."

My heart began pounding again.

That phrase.

It kept coming up.

And three months ago... no one had ever said it to me.

I ignored it.

"What else do you know about my mother?" I asked. "She was taken by a vampire. Do you know who?"

He closed his eyes briefly, resting his fingers against his chin as if thinking.

"There has been talk," he said after a moment. "Rumors."

My focus sharpened.

"It is believed your mother was not taken by an ordinary vampire... but by a pureblood."

A pureblood?

What the hell was that?

I thought vampires were just... vampires.

"You seem confused," he said. "A pureblood is the strongest type of vampire. Unlike others, they possess no trace of human blood. They are born as vampires—completely pure."

He continued calmly.

"However, they are not the most dangerous. Their hunger is far more controlled than that of common vampires, due to their experience and lineage."

I studied him more closely now.

Something about him stood out.

"What about you?" I asked. "What kind are you?"

He smirked slightly—his first real expression.

"I am a pureblood," he said. "If that's what you were wondering."

Chapter Eleven

This was beyond nerve-wracking.

I was face to face with a pureblood vampire.

If everything he said was true, then he was stronger than the vampire I had fought... stronger than Karma. This guy could rip my head off with a flick of his hand—something that would feel effortless to him.

He could tear my heart out faster than a single heartbeat. He could drain me dry before I even realized what was happening.

Who knew what he was truly capable of?

The thought alone froze me. I didn't even want to swallow the saliva building in my mouth.

A bead of sweat rolled down my face, hitting the ground harder than it should have.

The vampire in front of me raised his hands in a casual, surrendering gesture—now wearing a soft smile.

"Calm down," he said gently. "I wouldn't harm a fly."

I didn't believe him.

Instead, I tightened my grip on my dagger, forcing myself to stay composed. I couldn't back down—not when I was this close to answers about my mother.

"This pureblood vampire," I pressed. "Does he have a name?"

He lowered his hands.

"Speaking of names... I didn't catch yours," he replied.

"Why does that matter?" I shot back.

"It's only polite," he said calmly. "Especially since I'm the one giving you information."

He had a point.

As much as I hated it, I needed him.

"Dawn," I said. "My name is Dawn."

"Nice to meet you, Dawn," he replied. "I am Lyserg."

"Now—my mother," I pushed.

Lyserg paused briefly before answering.

"His name is Astral," he said. "That is all I know. Whoever he is, he doesn't stay in one place for long. He doesn't belong to any faction."

He continued,

"Most vampires—unless they are rogue or newly turned—join factions. It is illegal, especially for a pureblood, to remain unaffiliated. Factions keep our society organized. Each one is led by an elder vampire responsible for maintaining order."

A slight pause.

"I belong to the Rain faction."

"Damn it," I muttered, glancing down.

Just like that... another dead end.

I had finally gotten a lead—only to hit another wall.

"I'll keep an ear out for more information about your mother," Lyserg added.

For a moment, his words sparked something unfamiliar in me.

Hope.

It clashed against everything I believed about vampires.

Were they really all monsters?

...No.

They had to be.

Nothing good could come from something that fed on people.

"Well," Lyserg said, shifting slightly, "I should be heading to class. I'd rather not be late."

Still cautious, I let him turn his back first. I watched him carefully as he began to walk away.

But after a few steps, he stopped.

"Oh—and one more thing," he said without turning around.

"Be careful who you keep close to you. You're beginning to carry a scent... one that resembles a vampire's."

My chest tightened.

"If I were you," he continued, "I'd inform the principal. You're changing."

Changing?

No.

No way.

I hadn't been bitten. There was no way I was turning into a vampire.

He had to be lying.

I watched as Lyserg disappeared into the distance.

But I couldn't move.

I stood there, trapped in my own thoughts—looping through confusion, fear, and doubt.

He was a pureblood.

He seemed to know too much.

Either everything he said was true...

Or he had just fed me the perfect lie.

But why lie to me?

I was nothing to him.

And if he wasn't lying...

Then what was happening to me?

My parents weren't vampires.

And if my mother really was a hunter...

Then she spent her life killing things like him.

So what did that make me?

The question alone sent a chill through my body.

Was I really becoming...

The very thing I feared most?

Chapter Twelve

Days had passed since I last saw Luna.

I wanted—no, needed—to see her.

She was the only place I felt safe. Since coming to this school, I'd felt outmatched—surrounded by darkness in the form of vampires. But when I was with Luna, it felt like I wasn't alone.

Like I still had something real.

The time we spent together felt like childhood all over again—when nothing mattered except being ourselves.

Now... that feeling was slipping away.

She was fading from me.

Again.

And the thought that I might become a vampire—

That I might never be able to stand beside her again—

It dragged me deeper into something I couldn't escape.

How could I ever face her... knowing the line between human and vampire was blurring inside me?

A knock came at my bedroom door.

"Come in," I called from my bed, already knowing it was Hendrix.

He stepped in, leaving the door open.

"The principal wants to see you," he said.

...Crap.

This had to be about the vampire dorm.

Someone must've seen me. But when? Which time?

My nerves spiked instantly.

Honestly, I would've preferred the discipline office.

What did the principal want with me? What was the punishment for crossing into vampire territory?

My thoughts spiraled as I forced myself to stand and head toward his office.

When I got there, I stopped outside the door.

I didn't knock.

I didn't move.

People passed by, but I didn't care. My legs felt like they would give out beneath me. I needed to steady myself—just enough to walk in without falling apart.

For a moment... I thought about running.

Just turning around and going back to my room.

But then what?

That wasn't a plan—it was just delay.

And eventually, he'd send someone for me anyway.

Before I could think any further—

The door opened.

I was done.

I walked in without thinking, my body moving on its own. Fear dragged me forward like I had no control left. I didn't even look at who opened the door.

My focus stayed locked on the principal.

His expression confirmed everything.

He knew.

The door closed behind me, but I didn't turn around. I just stood there, staring at him as he stared back in silence.

"You called me here?" I asked, my voice cracking despite my attempt to stay calm.

"Yes," he replied.

A pause.

Then suddenly—his expression changed.

"Cheer up," he said with a light tone. "You're not in any trouble."

Relief hit me instantly.

So strong that I finally turned—

And froze.

Luna stood beside me.

Wearing a campus security uniform.

The same one Karma wore.

She stood tall, composed—like a trained hunter. Like someone who belonged here.

"Luna?" I muttered.

She glanced at me briefly, offering a faint, forced smirk before looking back at the principal.

It wasn't real.

I could tell.

She was still uncomfortable around me.

And that...

That hurt more than anything.

She looked at me differently now.

Like I had lost her trust.

Like I wasn't the same person anymore.

"Luna has been placed in the hunter division," the principal explained. "After a series of evaluations, she has officially passed."

I didn't respond.

I couldn't.

I just kept watching her—watching her avoid looking at me.

"You're probably wondering what this has to do with you," he continued. "Luna has informed me that you may be undergoing a transformation... into a vampire."

"What?" I snapped, cutting him off.

"Dawn, hear him out," Luna said softly.

Her voice calmed me instantly.

Even now... she still had that effect on me.

"As I was saying," the principal continued, "under normal circumstances, you would be transferred to the night dorm."

My jaw tightened.

"But Luna has requested an alternative solution—one I've only approved once before."

I listened carefully.

"She has requested that you remain in the day dorm... at least until your transformation is complete."

I glanced at Luna, a small smile forming despite everything.

She was trying to help me.

Even after everything.

"The condition," the principal continued, "is that Luna will be responsible for you. She will monitor your behavior, ensure you attend all classes, and report any irregularities."

My expression slowly faded.

"There's more," he added. "To make this arrangement possible, we've reassigned your roommate. Hendrix will remain where he is. You, however, will be moved to a new dorm."

A pause.

"It is a two-bedroom unit."

Another pause.

"But instead of another male..."

He looked between us.

"Luna will be your roommate."

My brain stopped.

Luna... and I... living together?

This wasn't a punishment.

This was something else entirely.

And somehow...

That made it worse.

Because I knew what this meant.

She still cared about me.

And I cared about her.

And if I really was changing—

Then I could hurt her.

She was putting herself at risk... for me.

Which meant I should've refused.

I should've said no.

But I couldn't.

I didn't speak.

Didn't move.

I just stood there—accepting it.

"Understand this," the principal continued. "This arrangement has failed before. The difference is... neither party was a hunter."

His tone sharpened.

"Luna—your reputation is now on the line. If you violate any terms, you will be stripped of your title and punished to the highest extent of academy law."

He paused.

"Sixty days. Twenty-three hours a day in detention. Followed by judgment from the hunter council."

Silence filled the room.

"Do you both understand?"

Luna didn't hesitate.

She answered immediately.

Sealing her fate.

And placing her life...

In my hands.

Chapter Thirteen

I waited outside the principal's office while Luna stayed inside talking with him. I tried to tune out what I could hear, focusing instead on the trouble I was putting her through.

I really thought she was going to abandon me after the night I scared her with my eyes.

But instead...

She had been looking out for me this entire time.

I still couldn't believe how much she cared.

Luna didn't stay long. She stepped out with a closed-mouth smirk, avoiding eye contact as she approached me.

I understood.

I wasn't about to blame her for feeling uneasy. I probably would've felt the same way if I were assigned to monitor someone turning into a vampire.

Because if everyone was right...

It was only a matter of time before I craved blood.

Before I lost control.

Before I hurt someone.

...Before I hurt her.

We walked in silence toward the couples' dorms—our new home. Luna didn't say a word.

Honestly, the silence worked in our favor. No one would overhear us.

Relationships on campus were forbidden unless the couple was married. Because of that, most students relied on something called Time Away—scheduled time where they were escorted off campus by a hunter to meet someone from the outside world. It was allowed once a month, with approval from the attendance office.

There were only a few married couples on campus—three that I knew of. Once married, they were placed in small housing units near the main office.

The couples' dorms were located near the campus entrance, while the main office sat in the center of the school.

As we approached the dorm, Luna finally spoke—her voice low.

"The principal wants us to act like a couple," she said. "That way, no one suspects anything... and you won't have to move to the vampire dorm. At least not yet."

Act like a couple?

Damn it.

How was I supposed to pretend with Luna... without letting my real feelings slip out?

This was a terrible idea.

We stopped in front of the door. Without thinking, I asked,

"Are you okay with this?"

Luna's hand paused on the doorknob. Her expression shifted—like she had slipped into deep thought.

Did my question remind her of that night?

"Dawn," she said, finally looking at me.

Her eyes locked onto mine.

"You're my friend. A close friend. I've known you since we were kids."

A small pause.

"I'll always have your back."

I could feel the truth in her words.

She meant it.

She still cared.

I nodded, smiling slightly as she opened the door.

"I'll take care of you," she added.

Those words hit harder than anything else.

Because they proved exactly what I was afraid of.

I couldn't do this.

I couldn't risk her life like this.

I couldn't become the thing that destroyed her.

I watched as she walked inside, setting the keys on the kitchen counter like everything was normal—like she wasn't moving in with someone who might turn into a monster.

She turned back and looked at me.

"Are you coming in, silly?" she teased.

Her warmth gave me just enough courage to step inside. I closed the door behind me.

"Sorry," I said.

"Don't be. Make yourself at home," she replied.

I sat on the couch while she stood at the edge of the kitchen, watching me.

Something was on her mind.

"What's wrong?" I asked.

She sighed.

"I got my first assignment today."

"Yeah... sorry you have to watch me," I said.

"No—that's not it," she replied.

She hesitated.

"Students have been going missing. Human students."

My posture straightened.

"The school is trying to keep it quiet, but people are starting to notice."

"So what—there's a rogue vampire?" I asked. "Did someone finally lose control?"

"No," she said. "There are signs a vampire is involved… but whoever it is, they're careful. They're covering their tracks."

She paused.

"The principal assigned me a partner. Someone more experienced. We're supposed to investigate together."

"I'm going with you," I said immediately.

Her expression hardened.

"I won't let you do this alone," I continued. "Even if you have a partner—I'll be there. I've got your back, just like—"

"No," she cut in.

"You don't owe me anything. I can handle this."

She was serious.

But I wasn't backing down.

"The investigation starts tonight," she added. "I'll keep you updated."

"No," I said firmly. "I'm going. That's final."

She opened her mouth—but I kept going.

"It's not about owing you. I want to be there for you. When I left before, I didn't have a choice. But now I do—and I'm not leaving you again."

I took a step closer.

"Besides... three is better than two."

She hesitated.

Then finally—

"Okay," she said. "But don't make my job harder than it already is."

Chapter Fourteen

Evening settled in as Luna and I stood in the center of campus, waiting for our third member.

My patience was wearing thin. We had already been standing there for twenty minutes.

That rogue vampire could be attacking its next victim right now... while we waited on a no-show hunter.

"Why can't we just start without them?" I asked. "Aren't we just searching the school?"

"No," Luna replied. "We're leaving campus. And to do that, we need a higher-ranking hunter with us."

"Why leave campus if the attacks are happening in the human dorm?"

"A rogue vampire doesn't stay far from its feeding grounds," she explained. "Since it's been attacking here every night, this is its hunting area. So we'll be searching just outside school grounds—for its nest."

"And where do we start?"

"Dark, abandoned places. Anywhere a vampire could hide during the day—caves, sewers... places like that. There's a sewer line nearby. That's our first stop."

This was it.

My first real chance to kill a vampire.

To start avenging my mother.

To rid the world of the disease these creatures spread.

And maybe...

Just maybe...

I could get answers.

If this vampire knew anything—if it had any connection to the one who took my mother—

I'd make it talk.

My hand hovered near the dagger at my hip.

I was ready.

...Or at least, I thought I was.

"There she is," Luna said, pointing toward the vampire dorm.

My heart started pounding.

This was really happening.

As the figure approached, I recognized her.

Karma.

The same hunter who had beaten me down not too long ago.

"Long time no see, pal," Karma said, resting a hand on her hip. "Looks like you took my advice about the night dorm."

Before I could respond, Luna looked between us.

"You two know each other?"

"Of course we do," Karma said with a smirk. "Don't we, buddy?"

"I met her once," I said shortly.

"He means I kicked his ass," Karma corrected. "He walked into vampire territory making demands—so I showed him exactly who was in charge."

I clenched my fists.

I was ready for a rematch.

Last time, I held back.

This time... I wouldn't.

"Oh," Luna said. "Don't feel bad. If you fought Karma and lost, that's normal. She's one of the best hand-to-hand combat hunters here."

...Great.

Now Luna knew.

I exhaled sharply, pushing it aside. I didn't have time for this.

"Can we get moving?" I snapped.

Karma laughed at my irritation.

"Sure," she said casually.

That attitude of hers—like everything was a joke—was starting to get on my nerves. She could fool Luna, but not me.

"Alright, team," Karma said, clapping her hands once. "First things first—do you both have your hunter weapons?"

I was surprised she didn't question why I was even here. I wasn't a hunter. She should've made a bigger deal about it.

Maybe she wanted to see me struggle.

Or fail.

"Yes, ma'am," Luna replied, showing the pink pistol holstered at her hip.

I still couldn't believe she was a hunter. She had never been the fighting type...

But maybe losing her brother changed that.

"Good," Karma said. "Let's move. The principal doesn't want us out too late."

Chapter Fifteen

I was outside the academy grounds for the first time in three months.

I felt like a stranger to the outside world.

But nothing had changed.

Cars still filled the streets. People moved about their lives, heading home from work like any other day.

Not far from the school, an empty park stood between us and the road. To anyone watching, it would've looked like we had just walked out of the woods—thanks to the spell concealing the academy.

Luna had already told me we wouldn't be going far. If the attacks were happening on school grounds, then the nest had to be nearby.

We walked casually through the park, blending in like three normal people enjoying the evening. The sunset cast a calm glow over everything—completely opposite of what we were here to do.

Following the sidewalk, we eventually reached a sewer entrance.

Luna stayed alert behind us as Karma and I lifted the lid. It was already loose.

"Ladies first," I said.

Karma smirked and climbed down the ladder without hesitation.

Luna followed next.

"Be careful," I told her.

She smiled back before descending.

I went last, pulling the lid shut above us.

The moment my feet touched the damp ground, Karma spoke.

"Looks like someone has a crush."

I ignored her.

So did Luna.

Looking ahead, there were two paths—but only one mattered. A trail of blood smeared along the walls marked the way forward.

Whoever this vampire was...

They were messy.

"Stay sharp," Karma warned. "Judging by the blood, this isn't just any vampire. This is a newcomer."

"What's that?" I asked, keeping my voice low.

"A newly turned vampire," Luna answered. "Less than a year old. Their first year is the worst—they can't control themselves. They feed constantly."

Karma added,

"And because they feed so much, they're stronger and faster than most. Blood fuels their power."

She cracked her knuckles.

"If we run into it, aim for the legs first. Slow it down. That's the only way we take it out."

For once, I didn't argue.

We moved deeper into the tunnels in silence.

The only sounds were dripping water and the distant creaking of old pipes above us. The tunnels were wide—plenty of room to fight if it came to that.

This was my first real hunt.

All I had to go off of were horror movies.

I scanned the darkness, half-expecting to find a coffin.

But the deeper we went...

The worse it got.

The smell of death grew stronger.

And then we saw them.

Body parts.

Scattered.

Torn apart like they meant nothing.

I could feel Luna tensing beside me.

I felt it too.

But Karma didn't react at all.

"Don't look," she warned.

We both obeyed, forcing our eyes forward.

Then—

A scream.

Sharp.

Inhuman.

It echoed through the tunnels, freezing us in place.

It was close.

Too close.

Karma moved first.

She rushed forward, pulling out her brass knuckles—lined with claw-like blades.

Luna followed, drawing her pink pistol.

I pulled my dagger and sprinted after them.

"We need to reach it before it leaves the nest!" Karma shouted.

We didn't have to go far.

Just one sharp turn—

And there it was.

Standing only a few meters ahead.

No coffin.

No hiding place.

Just a figure.

Waiting.

The creature turned toward us.

Its eyes locked onto ours—

And it screamed again.

A battle cry.

Then it lunged.

We were its next meal.

Chapter Sixteen

The creature was faster than I expected—reaching all three of us in an instant.

Up close, I could see it clearly.

The vampire... was a woman.

Her clothes were torn and filthy, barely holding together like scraps of cloth clinging to her body. What once might've been a thin red dress now hung loosely over her frail frame.

Karma didn't hesitate.

She struck first—her fist colliding with the vampire's face with a sharp crack that echoed through the tunnel.

The vampire hit the ground, her hair falling over her face.

But she didn't stay down.

In a blur, she sprang back up—moving faster than my eyes could track.

Only Karma seemed able to follow her movements.

The vampire rushed her again.

Karma reacted instantly, grabbing both of her wrists mid-attack and locking them in place. The vampire's sharp nails hovered inches from Karma's face as the two struggled.

Karma held her—but she couldn't attack.

Which meant the opening was ours.

Luna moved first.

I followed close behind—but I forced myself to think. One wrong move could get her—or Karma—killed.

Luna couldn't fire her weapon. They were too close.

She was going in for hand-to-hand combat.

No.

I surged forward, overtaking her with my dagger raised.

Closing the distance, I swung—aiming to sever the vampire's arm.

But somehow...

She knew.

Without even looking at me, the vampire reacted—using her speed to pull herself and Karma out of range. My blade cut through nothing but air.

Realizing she was at a disadvantage, the vampire thrashed violently—like a wild animal.

Karma's grip broke.

The vampire shoved her back, sending Karma crashing into the wall.

But Karma recovered instantly.

She stood again, ready.

Unshaken.

The vampire lunged once more—

And Karma met her with a sharp jab to the face.

That's when everything changed.

The vampire snapped.

She began ricocheting off the walls at terrifying speed—too fast to track.

All Luna and I could see were afterimages.

She was everywhere.

Behind us.

Above us.

In front of us.

Then—gone again.

There was no way to predict her next move.

Karma was ready.

We weren't.

I definitely wasn't.

Then—

She chose.

Her target…

Was me.

Before I could react, she appeared in front of me.

Her hand wrapped around my throat.

And in the next instant—

I was slammed against the wall.

Lifted off the ground.

Her grip tightened.

Crushing.

My air vanished.

My body struggled—but it was useless.

Luna and Karma's voices echoed faintly in the distance… but they sounded so far away.

Everything blurred.

Then—

I saw her face.

Up close.

Pale.

Sunken.

Twisted by hunger.

The face of a monster.

The face of a killer.

The face of—

My mother.

My heart stopped.

No...

No, that wasn't possible.

But it was.

Even with her hollow cheeks...

Even with those red, blood-starved eyes...

Her blonde hair...

Her features...

It was her.

"M... Mom..." I choked out, tears instantly filling my eyes.

Her grip loosened.

Her expression changed.

Recognition.

I saw it.

She knew me.

Tears formed in her eyes too.

She was still in there.

Still fighting.

Still... my mother.

And just as her hand began to release me—

A gunshot rang out.

The sound exploded through the tunnel.

Both of us froze.

Neither of us knew—

Who had been hit.

And in that moment...

I found myself hoping—

It was me.

Chapter Seventeen

Blood dripped—making everything painfully clear.

The bullet had hit my mother in the side of her stomach.

She released me, and I dropped to the ground.

Looking at the wound, I saw blood pouring out fast. Normally, a vampire would heal almost instantly...

But not from a hunter's weapon.

She was bleeding out.

My mother glanced down at her wound for a moment before lifting her eyes back to me.

There was sadness in them.

The kind only a parent could show... right before doing something their child wouldn't understand.

"Aim for the head," Karma called out from behind me.

My head snapped toward her.

"Luna, don't—it's my mom!" I shouted.

Luna's expression shifted instantly—shock, confusion, disbelief—as she lowered her weapon.

That moment of hesitation—

Was all it took.

My mother moved.

In a flash, she was on Karma—her teeth sinking into her neck.

Karma screamed, struggling to pry her off—but she couldn't.

From the angle I saw, my mother had a perfect grip.

If we didn't act now...

Karma was dead.

I forced myself up, ignoring the pain, sprinting toward them.

"Let her go!" I shouted.

But Luna made the call.

She fired.

Two shots—straight into my mother's back.

The wounds sizzled, smoke rising from where the bullets struck.

My mother released Karma.

Her scream filled the tunnels—raw, agonizing, inhuman.

She arched back, her body trembling as pain tore through her.

I could hear it.

Feel it.

Right in front of me...

She was dying.

Without thinking, I threw myself in front of her—arms spread wide.

A shield.

Protecting her.

From them.

But was I making the right choice?

She was a vampire now.

She could attack again.

She could kill Luna.

Kill Karma.

We could end it here.

End her suffering.

End the threat.

My mind had the answer.

She's not your mother anymore.

But my heart—

My heart shattered.

I didn't find her just to lose her again.

I didn't come this far just to watch her die.

Tears streamed down my face.

"Stop..." I choked. "Please... that's enough."

My voice broke—but I meant every word.

I couldn't let them hurt her anymore.

Luna lowered her weapon completely.

I knew she would.

She couldn't shoot—with me standing in the way.

I saw the pain in her eyes.

The conflict.

The guilt.

Tears began forming in her eyes too.

Karma staggered toward her, clutching her bleeding neck.

"Dawn... move," she ordered. "Mother or not—she has to be stopped."

"No!" I snapped. "I won't let anyone hurt her!"

Silence followed.

My mother's screams had faded into weak, pained whimpers.

"There has to be another way," I said, my voice trembling. "Can't we take her back? To the academy? Help her somehow?"

"And bring her back to the same place where she killed students?" Karma shot back. "No, Dawn. She has to be stopped."

I hesitated.

Because I knew what I was about to say.

And what it meant.

It meant going against the academy.

Against the hunters.

Against everything.

But I couldn't live with myself if I let them kill her.

"Then you'll have to shoot me first," I said.

My voice steadied.

Despite everything.

"I'm not moving."

Chapter Eighteen

There was no response.

Only silence.

Only a standoff.

My former allies stood in front of me, and I stood in their line of fire—risking my life, trusting my childhood friend not to pull the trigger just to kill my mother.

My eyes locked onto Luna's—the one holding the gun.

They were filled with sorrow.

I could see it breaking her.

But I also saw her decision.

She wasn't going to shoot.

Karma didn't move either.

No command.

No attack.

I exhaled slowly, releasing the tension that had been crushing my chest.

I was about to speak—about to apologize, ready to face whatever consequences the academy would throw at me—

When everything changed.

A black trench coat flashed between them.

Too fast to follow.

Before I could react—

Karma was sent flying.

Her body shot past me, her scream echoing through the tunnel before she slammed into the ground headfirst.

She didn't move.

I didn't know if she was alive.

I didn't have time to check.

My attention snapped back to Luna.

Seconds passed—

But it felt like forever.

Then—

Impact.

A pale foot slammed into Luna's chest, launching her into the wall.

Her back hit hard.

A sharp grunt escaped her as she clutched her spine, her eyes squeezing shut in pain.

I still couldn't see him.

He was too fast.

So I stopped relying on my eyes.

I moved.

Charging toward Luna, I swung my blade wildly through the air—hoping his speed would betray him, hoping he'd run straight into it.

I was almost there—

Then a hand struck my chest.

Not a hit—

A push.

But the force behind it...

It lifted me off my feet.

I was thrown backward like I weighed nothing, my body dragged through the air before slamming onto the sewer floor.

I skidded through the shallow water.

Pain exploded through my back.

I forced myself up—

And froze.

Luna was in the air.

Dangling.

Held by her throat.

A pale vampire stood there, shirtless—his grip tight around her neck.

His smile...

Cold.

Amused.

He was enjoying this.

This guy...

He was even faster than my mother.

I glanced toward her.

She wasn't moving.

Just watching.

And the look on her face—

She knew him.

She wasn't a threat anymore.

She had surrendered.

That told me everything.

I ran.

Full speed.

If he wanted to toy with me, fine.

That was his mistake.

Because that meant Luna was still alive.

Still had a chance.

I swung my dagger the moment I got close—

But he didn't even look at me.

Without releasing Luna, he backhanded me.

I hit the ground instantly.

Got back up just as fast.

No hesitation.

I lunged again—this time aiming for his side.

He shifted—his entire body slipping out of range like smoke.

Gone.

Then—behind me.

I turned, following the wind brushing against my neck.

He still held Luna.

Her movements were slowing.

Her strength fading.

I thrust forward—

But before my attack could land—

A punch.

Straight to my face.

Everything blurred.

My body gave out—

But I didn't hit the ground.

He caught me.

By my shirt.

Pulled me forward.

Held me there.

Face to face.

His eyes...

Pitch black.

Empty.

No hunger.

No mercy.

Just cruelty.

A monster.

Dark blue hair framing his face.

Then—

He threw me.

My body slammed into the wall like a missile, pain ripping through my side as I dropped to the ground.

For a moment, everything spun.

Then my vision cleared.

And I looked up.

He was still holding Luna.

His full attention on her now.

That same smile.

Death.

Luna was barely moving.

She was losing.

She was dying.

Right in front of me.

"Come on, Dawn," he called out casually. "You'll have to be faster than that if you want to save your little girlfriend."

My body wouldn't move.

Not fast enough.

Not strong enough.

First my mother...

Now Luna.

Because I was too weak.

Again.

"P-please..." I begged, my voice breaking. "Don't kill her..."

He ignored me.

Completely.

Then—

He spoke.

"You've been searching for your mother..."

A pause.

"For me."

My heart stopped.

"And now that I've finally shown myself..."

His grip tightened slightly.

"You're just going to stand there again... while I take someone else you love?"

Silence.

Everything inside me...

Broke.

And something else—

Something darker—

Woke up.

Chapter Nineteen

I felt nothing.

Not my thoughts.

Not my fear.

Not even my own actions.

Before I realized what had happened...

Luna was in my arms.

Unconscious—but alive.

Breathing.

I had saved her.

At some point... I had moved her away from him.

The vampire who had held her moments ago now stood at a distance.

His hand—

The one that had gripped her throat—

Was gone.

Severed.

Lying on the ground.

Blood pooled beneath it.

The smile that once stretched across his face was gone.

Replaced with confusion... as he stared at what remained of his arm.

I gently lowered Luna against the wall behind me.

Then I turned back to him.

I didn't feel anything.

No hesitation.

No fear.

Only purpose.

"So it was you who took my mother from me... right?" I asked calmly.

His eyes snapped toward me—but he said nothing.

I took a step forward.

Then another.

"And you're the one who turned her into this monster... aren't you?"

Still no answer.

But I didn't need one.

Even from where I stood, I could see the fear on my mother's face.

She knew him.

"If ruining my life wasn't enough…" I continued, my voice colder than I had ever heard it, "you tried to take the only good thing I had left."

My eyes hardened.

"Luna."

A pause.

"I know you won't answer me."

Another step forward.

"So I'll just kill you."

I moved.

He didn't even see it coming.

In an instant, I was beside him—my hand striking his throat, followed by a crushing punch to his stomach.

He folded.

Too slow.

Too weak.

As he tried to recover, I slipped behind him—

And drove my hand straight through his back.

Like his body was water.

His flesh gave way under my fingers.

Cold blood spilled out as he jerked, a sharp scream tearing from his throat.

I ripped my hand free—

Then hurled him across the tunnel.

His body slammed into the wall, cracking it on impact.

He dropped—but forced himself back up.

Barely.

His shoulder hung out of place, the bone pressing dangerously against his skin.

His body was already trying to heal.

Slowly.

Pathetically.

I watched him.

And for the first time...

I understood the feeling.

The thrill of power.

Of watching something helpless beneath you.

Like prey.

Like he had done to us.

"Do you really think I'm going to let you heal?" I asked, my voice dark—almost unrecognizable.

I stepped forward again.

Ready to finish him.

To make him suffer.

But then—

It hit me.

The feeling vanished.

The numbness.

Gone.

Fear rushed back in.

My heart slammed against my chest.

My body felt... normal again.

Too normal.

Too slow.

I saw it immediately.

I wasn't moving like before.

Not even close.

And then—

That smile.

His smile.

It was back.

Before I could react—

Something pierced my neck.

I froze.

Looking down, I saw them.

His fingers.

Three of them.

Buried deep in my throat.

Warmth spread instantly from the wound.

"You should've killed me when you had the chance," he whispered coldly.

He pulled his hand free.

My body dropped.

I hit the ground hard, landing on my side.

I couldn't move.

Not a single muscle.

Cold crept through me.

My vision blurred.

Everything started to fade.

Then his voice—

Close.

Too close.

"Go ahead…" he said.

"Feed on the girls."

My vision darkened.

The edges collapsing inward.

And just before everything went black—

I saw my mother's feet step past me.

Toward them.

No…

She—

Chapter Twenty

Mom... run.

I won't let anyone hurt you ever again.

This time... I'll protect you.

I'll protect everyone.

I stood face to face with the vampire.

Somehow, I had survived his attack to my neck.

His dark smile matched his shadowy eyes—no fear, no hesitation.

And somehow...

His hand had grown back.

I couldn't beat him.

I was hopeless.

No dagger.

No plan.

We were going to die.

He lunged at me—

My eyes shot open.

I jolted upright, grabbing at nothing, drenched in sweat.

"MOM!" I shouted—

But another voice answered instead.

"Dawn, Dawn—it's okay. It's okay."

Pain shot through my neck. My throat burned, raw and sore from that single word.

I looked around.

A wall in front of me.

A bed beneath me.

Then I turned to my left.

Luna.

She sat beside me in a chair pulled close to the bed, her face filled with relief.

Before I could say anything, she jumped up and wrapped her arms around me—holding me tightly, like I might disappear if she let go.

Without thinking, I hugged her back.

The last thing I remembered...

My mother had been ordered to kill us.

And yet—

Here we were.

Alive.

In the nurse's office.

A private room.

Her grip tightened until the pain forced me to speak.

"Luna... easy," I said gently.

She pulled back quickly, her face turning red.

My voice came out raspy.

Instinctively, I reached for my neck—but thick bandages stopped me.

Along with the ones already wrapped around my chest and stomach, someone had patched me up well.

The school nurse, most likely.

Then I noticed Luna.

The mark around her neck.

Clear.

Dark.

A handprint.

My chest tightened.

I tried to focus on her face—but my eyes kept drifting back to it.

I had failed her.

"I wasn't sure when you'd wake up," Luna said softly. "Karma kept telling me you'd be fine... but I couldn't stop worrying."

I forced a small laugh.

"Guess she was right."

But I couldn't meet her eyes.

That mark...

It said everything.

"Dawn."

Her hand lifted my chin, forcing me to look at her.

"We're alive. That's what matters."

She knew.

Of course she did.

I nodded.

"You're right."

But it didn't change anything.
She almost died.

Because I wasn't strong enough.

If Karma hadn't been there...

We would've been dead long before the other vampire showed up.

"So... Karma was here?" I asked.

"Yeah," Luna said. "But she had to report to the principal."

I looked down at the sheets.

"Don't worry," she added quickly. "She said she's not going to tell him about what you did with your mom."

That wasn't what I was worried about.

Still, I smiled.

"That's... nice of her."

The words scratched painfully through my throat.

Luna stood.

"We're home now," she said gently. "You should rest. I'll make you some soup."

Right.

Our dorm.

I had almost forgotten.

She walked into the kitchen, moving like everything was normal.

But nothing was normal.

A thought hit me.

"How did we get out of the sewer?" I called out.

"Karma used a garlic bomb," Luna answered from the kitchen. "The vampires ran. That's what she told me."

I exhaled quietly.

Yeah...

I owed Karma.

Big time.

From where I sat, I could see Luna moving around the kitchen.

Then I noticed it—

Another bruise.

Just below her collarbone.

Where she'd been kicked.

She looked... happy.

Focused on taking care of me.

Like none of it mattered.

But it did.

This was my fault.

My mother had almost killed them.

And the vampire who took her...

He was still out there.

If what he said was true—

He was the one behind everything.

And now my mother...

Was a monster.

A hunter's target.

Which meant...

It was only a matter of time before someone else found her.

And killed her.

That left me with one choice.

I had to do it first.

I had to kill my mother.

Before they could.

And after that—

I would kill the monster who made her this way.

No matter what.

No matter who stood in my way.

Even if that meant going against the hunters themselves.

Don't miss out!

Visit the website below and you can sign up to receive emails whenever Sakari Lacross publishes a new book. There's no charge and no obligation.

https://books2read.com/r/B-A-GXQL-WMELB

BOOKS 2 READ

Connecting independent readers to independent writers.

Did you love *How Long Is Forever*? Then you should read *Burn Brothers*[1] by Sakari Lacross!

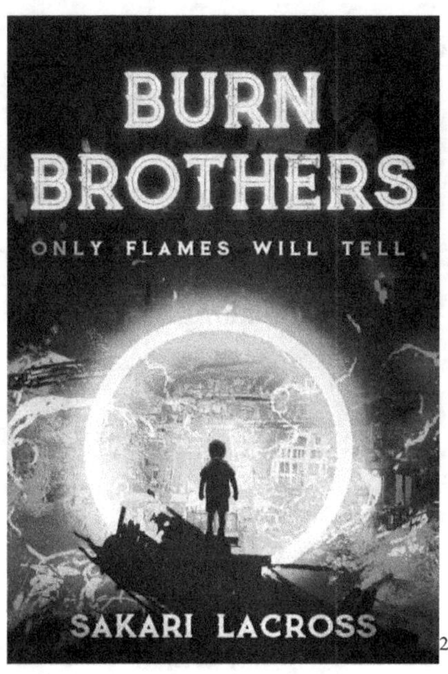

[2]

Jayk, a super-powered being with the ability to manifest and manipulate fire, has tried to keep his powers a secret. He has tried to live a normal life, living amongst mortals as he always intended. However, the one thing that he has run from, has finally caught up to him. A part of his past that could jepardize his future if it isn't stopped...his younger brother.

---

1. https://books2read.com/u/bWG2Q7

2. https://books2read.com/u/bWG2Q7

Also by Sakari Lacross

A Dawn Breaking Romance
Romance Dawn
Beyond Dawn
Dawning
Never Ending

A Final World
Rising Tides
Don't End Up Consumed
Don't End Up Consumed 2

Belonging
I Hope I Belong
I Hope I Belong Too

Call U When I Arrive